IMAGINE

Alison Lester

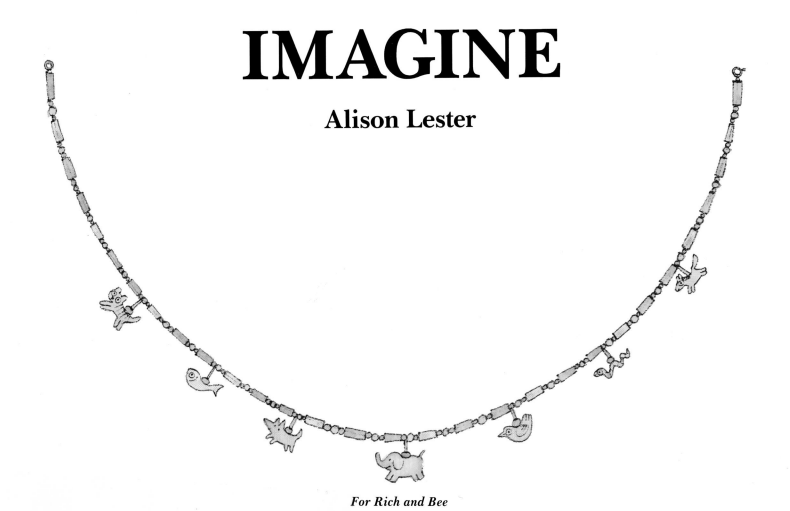

For Rich and Bee

Houghton Mifflin Company

Boston 1990

Imagine
if we were
deep in the jungle
where butterflies drift
and jaguars prowl
where parakeets squawk
and wild monkeys howl . . .

■

Imagine
if we were
like fish in the ocean
where anemones wave
and hammerheads glide
where seahorses rock
and hermit crabs hide . . .

∎

Imagine
if we were
crossing the icecap
where penguins toboggan
and arctic hares dash
where caribou snort
and killer whales crash . . .

■

humpback whale • narwhal • arctic dolphin • adele penguin • arctic hare

Imagine
if we were
out in the country
where horses gallop
and cattle graze
where turkeys gobble
and sheepdogs laze . . .

■

swan • duck • drake • duckling • rabbit • rooster • hen • chick • turkey • donkey • pig • piglet • fox

mouse • worm • crow • goose • cockatoo • swallow • puppy • sheep • goat

ouse • worm • crow • goose • pony • draughthorse • sheepdog • puppy • sheep • goat • swan • duck •

Imagine
if we were
surrounded by monsters
where pteranodons swoop
and triceratops smash
where stegosaurs stomp
and tyrannosaurs gnash . . .

■

Imagine
if we were
away on safari
where crocodiles lurk
and antelope feed
where leopards attack
and zebras stampede . . .

■

Imagine
if we were
alone in Australia
where bandicoots nibble
and wallabies jump
where wombats dig burrows
and kangaroos thump . . .

■

Imagine
if we had
our own little house
with a cat on the bed
a rug on the floor
a light in the night
and a dog at the door . . .

■

Imagine . . .